T0153325

FLESHGRAPHS

FLESHGRAPHS   BRYNNE REBELE-HENRY

Nightboat Books
New York

I.

I alphabetize the girls by tens and letters. First: Annie and her cellulite thighs that made her say of herself: walrus. I would bite them with my too sharp incisors. Second: Betty and the weird sounds she made that were more like birth than sex and her pinup rolled back hair. Third: Carrie, and her light moustache. Fourth: Diana and her autumn mouth and how she always burned cookies. I stop at six because that's too fucking sad but I think of her knuckles and the sound they made against my forehead still.

2.

The birth was a slick of fluids I never knew existed, the color spectrum on a palette of torn labia and mewls. My baby's face looks like a burned cat and I don't want to name this cartilage watermelon, this alien kitten. Instead I let it bite my torn nipples and sing lullabies in the language of my mother that I never bothered to know.

3.

Marco says, you like the girls, fucking them, I mean? I think, have you seen my haircut? And the way I know how to walk in strip clubs, how I know to hold my over-priced beer?

4.

Every time I sleep I dream of an abscess, usually on the side of my face. I squeeze and an explosion of pus, a tidal in my fingers and I don't like bandaids.

5.

I put on my wife's lipstick.

6.

You put your hand against my thigh. We both pretended it didn't happen.

7.

Sweep of brackish dripping down my legs, I don't like cotton so I push other things in it: the end of a silk scarf from a husband, a string of pearls, I think of fruits but I can't fit them, so I leave the stained twill bathmat and walk around my flat with the scarf and pearls flapping against my legs. Brandy's coming soon, she promised me cake.

8.

I loved you, the shape of the dark crescents of hair on your legs. I sweep my fingers into your ear, caviar-fingered, I sumptuous them into my mouth.

9.

He snarls when he is happy. I touch his underbelly like an incantation.

10.

She wrote me a letter and said to put my dick in the envelope. I'm thinking stamps and postal and the crisp white.

11.

Cocaine sunset, Jane says he did it off her nipples and it felt like summer. I think my mouth is too hot so I rub it on plastic, spread the bulky flesh of it with my fingers, I feel the crack of skin and the dry winter of it.

12.

I put vodka in my hair for kicks, then try to snort sugar. My eyes are a cesspool that cowboys could drown in.

13.

I didn't know what to say so I thought about kissing him and pulling the seafoam of his hair into my mouth.

14.

She touched my ankle, so I touched her neck, and then the spaces above and below it. And then she touched the bony expanse between my breasts and I thought about saying stop but instead decided to go on a scavenger hunt for places to bite: The space of her belly before her groin, her knee, the scar on her back that I lick, she laughs like a broken clock, and we both say enough to love.

15.

I like the parts of your body that show between the clothing,
I tell him.

16.

She takes a razor to her thighs and wrists in the shower and we
both pretend not to know. I listen outside, ear against oak for the
evidence of a vein split too far.

17.

I flinch during needles and sex scenes.

18.

I want to break my baby's bones, little and crunchy, to raise them into my mouth on a spit. Instead I suck the things he has sucked, pacifier, I tried my breast but it was too sagged and I couldn't reach so I fell back a dirty wilted plant and pretended to be a cave woman.

19.

When you come to the wet sad thing. I never work nights. A bathtub cut. I left my thong in his shower.

20.

When I kissed Baby Jones at a party I forgot to take out my retainer and he split my lip clean. He asked me to marry him later, biting his caterpillar mouth like a methed-out vampire. I said yes.

21.

He's almost a virgin, a slip of friction between hip bones was all it was, he tells me. I feel the static of hair bristle between my wrist and eye sockets.

22.

We all pretend not to see the birthmark splotches, the track marks down my arms. We just offer some concealer, maybe a sweater.

23.

I take a Sharpie to my breasts, arms, legs. I start to draw a map of London but then just make koala faces.

24.

She wanted to make me scream, a screw-driver, a curling iron, three jars of preserves and a lighter. "This is how we love now." Electric grid my thighs.

25.

I put my nose against yours and counted to four.

26.

I like the parts of the bodies of boys that don't connect, the galaxies of skin, their noses make bridges of star-burst cartilage. The way they bite their lips like dry fruits.

27.

For the metro-sexual: vanilla and tobacco. For the rich and unso-phisticated: faux cut grass. For the depressed: absinthe and musk.

28.

Sad sex on Fridays, a comet's discourse.

29.

We Christian girls put beeswax on our lips and holy water between our breasts and on our bellies. We tuck Jesus's body into our clothing. Discreet, we think.

30.

A slip of the razor, easy accident.

31.

I don't know what to wear, so I tie sage around my left ankle, twists of garlic in my hair. I want to be Italian and edible. I add rosemary, thyme. Frying oils.

32.

I brush my hair until it crackles onto the linoleum.

33.

She could feel the remains of him seeping out of her, radiation, she can feel her back beneath the mattress and it reminds her of Stonehenge. Reminds her of the tea she's left on her counter, steeping, the rim of black on the cup will be appearing around now.

34.

He sprays the cologne on his face. Diffusion.

35.

I wondered at the way her hair fell down in a clean black train, the tracks left on her face from yesterday's binder. I worry that she doesn't know my name or face, that she won't recognize, still dawning over her new hips and breasts. I say my name to the sound her arms make against the subway rails: Benji.

36.

The sad space girl Friday, the pseudo lesbian haircuts that sports moms flip backwards, too long nails though, Cheryl says, their mouths all dry and lipstick-chapsticked duo. Not enough velour, says I, with my chewed down wool, with my menthol smelling pockets, with my cuticles and nails so shot my fingers nudge through them.

37.

My virginity gone to a buck-toothed rabbit boy in a truck with a sleeping bag in the back and a window broke from holes torn in it by angry women who want to be girls, he says. It didn't feel like much but friction. After, my thighs were river banks for the blood. Next morning and bruise made sky from the seat-belt buckle.

38.

Her body washes in, a tangle of seaweed and her grandmother's fake sapphires. He is disappointed about the way her body is shaped. "I thought she was a whale." We watch her arching her back, her eyes sand-coated magnifying glasses. Ambulances never occur to us, we say later, when the light is a funeral home disco in our un-made-up faces. We just wanted to see some mating whales, we say.

39.

I lick the skin between her fingers.

40.

His skin is a weathered hollow of chemo, the spaces where he is deflating. We don't say anything about the liver spots, or the drowned white of his tremors. We just place toast inside our lips, chew.

41.

My girl's hair is dead, and her lips are a fine yellow. Chapped
nipples that I put in her throat, charred.

42.

His belly falls over his belt.

43.

My mother is disappearing.

44.

He pushes his thumb down Mary Anne's throat and says of it "Righteous."

45.

She brushes her oil-slick hair, polluted clumps, their follicles hail against the floor.

46.

He says he's just kissing invisible boys.

47.

He's all blues baby daddy, cat on a hot tin roof, double lashes. He wants it all deep fried and butter smothered with dirty sugar and maraschino cherries. His belt doesn't fit right and he punches extra holes into the thick skin of it with his rusty bottle opener.

48.

Lemons remind her too much of the bruises.

49.

The baby falls out every time she opens her legs, she tries to push him back in, this slippery disappearing child, she tries tight jeans, lying down until her spine makes railroads in the mattress. She calls for doctors, firemen, medicine witches, but she can't find a phone, she tries to call them on rotten fruits, all that's left in her cupboard.

50.

I'm shaking my hips and they all say of it: "That motherfucker's Beyoncé." They want to buy me shots, and I'm all "get in line, bitches," in my leather man-thong.

51.

My belly's bigger than my arms now, we run out of water five moons ago, Momma don't talk anymore, and Daddy's head went boom! when they come in with their sharp dust and guns, and all the animals want to eat me, says the leader, and our skin is falling off our bones, meaty no more.

52.

We walked to the mall, stroked our fingers over things we couldn't/ can't/won't afford. After, he pulled me against his chest and bit my neck. He touched his middle finger against the space between my eyebrows, then drew a cross over my mouth and nose. Then he bowed and skipped away.

53.

He pressed against her, concrete floor, a gun, maybe a knife, she doesn't remember. Ten months later and she's still bleeding. But they don't say rape or victim, instead their mouths form: antibiotics, tea, sympathy casseroles.

54.

Spray tan, he keeps saying things about me like divine, and baby, and scrumptious. Of my bikini: hot, hot, hot. His porno beard. His affinity for unicorn butt plugs and bedazzling.

55.

I fucked them in a car with no heat, it was winter and our skins made sweaty iced-over red-tinted sacks against each other. They called themselves Pedro and Bobby and bought me two blueberry Slurpees.

56.

The knife makes clean against my fingers. The tip of my thumb, almond sliver off my breasts, the round of my foot. All of the flesh my body doesn't need.

57.

He puts the gauge inside my nose, a needle that's too sharp, a blue stone. He says "Sweet spot found." Then pushes in until it crunches concave into my septum.

58.

All of us babies she didn't want/couldn't keep/a million reasons why. All of us babies, seven now, counting the new one popped out of dairy-like thighs. All of us wash our hair with two-dollar shampoo. All of us wear the same clothes, our bodies froglike. Doctor says tapeworm, the white thread that hangs out of us.

59.

He puts the condom on, still wearing the pig mask from last Halloween.

60.

She wonders where putting on Sharpie instead of lipstick would rank on the scale of taboo. She decides a 3, somewhere around a bloody tampon string hanging out of your shorts but not as bad as eating your hair/skin in public.

61.

Sarah and I go to the art party in dresses that make us look like beautiful aliens. Before we walk through the illuminated doorway, we drop the acid from London. Inside the gallery everyone is wearing weird headbands and eating cupcakes, we take some pastries and start crying because everything is so fucking pretty. A girl with Mickey Mouse ears looks at me and says: "You are cosmic." I think that touching her would be like conceiving with the universe, her breasts are glowing UFOs, and against her sequined t-shirt, they give off a sort of green light.

62.

His body is a husk of his former self, withered against the hospital sheets like a fossil nobody wanted to unearth.

63.

I didn't know what to do so I licked the side of his face.

64.

I buy concealer two shades darker than my skin to hide the bruises.

65.

The juice box bleeds over my hands when I see her back walking away.

66.

When they take away the knives, flatware, scissors, I start using pens, and when those are gone, my nails.

67.

What you do when the blinds are down and you have washed a bottle of Tide down with a bottle of whiskey and then licked the grime off all of your windows: you wait for the blunt needles to puncture your organs.

68.

I insert Exacto blades into the box of blue-black cupcakes and wait for the slicing in my belly.

69.

I asked my catholic school's P.E teacher if you can fuck a tree.

70.

A tongue isn't a tongue once you cut it out and cram it inside of every warm place you harbor.

71.

Queenie brings me bags of the magic powder and our brains turn
into submarines with holes in the sides.

72.

She wants to eviscerate my cunt.

73.

I tear my body apart with my fingers like an under-cooked chicken,
bland meat and juice running down my arms.

74.

David says that he knows what girls taste like: Sour cream and strawberries.

75.

I drink a cup of bleach and wait for my organs to turn shiny and blonde: beach bunny baby can't be acquired without pain but I know that every platinum dart of me will be fuckable.

76.

Barry said that threesomes are like the Father, Son and Holy Ghost gangbanging a communion wafer.

77.

Caroline is the only one who knows how to deep-throat.

78.

I plunge my fingers into her throat because I know that inside I will find rubies and some other shiny stones.

79.

He named his penis after his dead hamster.

80.

My grandmother swallows her five wedding rings like pills and says she can feel the ghosts of her ex-husbands inside of her again.

81.

The first time tasted like the ocean but the blood soaked through his mattress.

82.

My scars taste like boiled mystery meat.

83.

After service Emma and I fuck under the pews until our lipgloss and braces stick together, cherry-scented sparkle juice running into our teeth.

84.

Men are delicious candy stripes.

85.

The Whore House is painted the color of fleshy vulvas, and inside a mermaid with a cock asks if I want the salty seaman special.

86.

He said that he's buying me a drink and asks what's my poison's flavor so I tell him "pussy."

87.

I mix the overdone chicken thighs with butter cake and make soup out of it.

88.

He locked us in a storage facility to hibernate.

89.

Straight boys after dark aren't straight, just thin wavy sweat lines on the mattress.

90.

Catholic school is like one long gangbang, Lisa says.

91.

I try to fit a tin can inside of my mouth and the aluminum slices into my tongue like a piece of candy.

92.

Floral print is the new lingerie, she assures me.

93.

He wants to try anal fisting and I try to put my hand inside of him like a sexy doctor but he howls like a wounded sea animal.

94.

I'm not your average B rate whore: I can take it four ways and my cunt tastes like breakfast cereal.

95.

Grandpa takes an ax and buries it into his head and inside of his skull I find bits of gold dust from the Rush.

96.

Tendons taste like I Can't Believe It's Not Butter!

97.

Kesha tried to fuck a knife because she thought it would make her a god.

98.

Uncle has a thick wrist and a red car and a lot of candy and in the car he takes my clothes off and asks what I think of the other boys in my school and says not to be a fruit like him.

99.

I run my lipstick discolored teeth over her forearm until I can hear muscle shift and pop deliciously.

100.

Ray says sex tastes like over-cooked pasta.

101.

Jesus comes into the barn wearing a strap-on.

102.

I know what bones taste like: the salty hollow part of your elbow where bruises form.

103.

I take a vegetable peeler to my legs and the skin comes away in little strands.

104.

I sidle up to the cashier and undo the tie of my trench coat and my breasts come out and I rub them against the conveyor belt and lick my true love's face.

105.

I try to give myself a lesbian mullet but the scissors cut my scalp.

106.

I ask my wife if I can take a shit inside her.

107.

I lure them out with candy, bits of ribbon, who would suspect the young babysitter, the twelve-year-old fatherless bastard who goes to church three times a week and prays for your sins.

108.

I gargle her pussy juice and think "I am a sex smoothie machine."

109.

The new choir instructor is looking at me like I'm some sparkly abbed new boy candy that he can't wait to devour like a communion wafer and then pop my ass cherry but what he doesn't know is that I have sores that taste like citrus bitters and that can mean only one thing.

110.

Momma says to start with one finger for an hour everyday, and then to go up to all ten until it stretches out and I can take as many men as I want at once, because in her trade, she says, that's going to make you a bona fide millionaire.

111.

Her pubic hair crunches in my teeth.

112.

I tell her: love is when you want to drain her of her blood until her veins are brittle and you can crunch on them and eat her eyeballs and the inside of her mouth out with a grapefruit spoon and never get full no matter how much marrow you suck.

113.

He says enemas are in right now.

114.

My mother brings them home in droves, four men in the kitchen, two in the shower and one is drawing penises on our flowery wallpaper. I make a sandwich and wish for a thunderstorm.

115.

She said whips make it better.

116.

I crush the cherry blossoms from the tree in my yard and grind them into a paste, add three centipede legs and a dying caterpillar and stir it into her oolong tea.

117.

I tell him to bang me so hard my ovaries fall out.

118.

Cherry says childbirth is like an all-night one-night stand.

119.

First there was my wolf eyes, and then my arched backbone, hairy tits and legs, teeth that could gulp everything dry, and then the sleepless full moon and the blood on my thighs and mouth every morning.

120.

I twist my tongue into my trumpet's orifices.

121.

Her thighs taste like Lysol.

122.

I push my back against the pole, drop it low, and in my leopard print man-thong I am a dollar-stuffed demigod.

123.

She takes a pair of pliers to my molars and I wait for the pop and stab in my gums.

124.

He got so high last night he thought we were gay anteaters.

125.

She opens her mouth and a dead bird falls out.

126.

I try to carve the alphabet into my thighs with the sharp end of
a key.

127.

She cuts an illuminati sign into her belly and starts calling her-
self Lakshmi.

128.

Mary tells me to pretend that she's a bad puppy and parade her through the streets with a nipple ring leash.

129.

I do three lines and everything is bright and shiny as I step off the hotel roof and pretend to be a velociraptor.

130.

She bites my tongue and I try not to scream.

131.

Her pussy tastes like bad fish so I take a packet of soy sauce and squirt it inside her.

132.

I swallow three bullets and wash them down with paint varnish and wish I could be an angel, but as I wait for the wings to sprout out of me I think I can see a skull rippling in my stomach.

133.

He said to pretend to be George Bush and cum in his face.

134.

Three months and she still doesn't know it was just oregano, keeps telling everyone that she is the new Jesus.

135.

Two lines in and my nose is a glittery dolphin.

136.

I opened up my wrist and put electrical wires inside, waited for my whole body to light up like a million human lamps.

137.

I fuck everyone and my back can bend twenty degrees and my eyes can change color on demand.

138.

I told her to call me Daddy and to eat my old tampon.

139.

Sarai tried to eat a clock and now she says everything is turquoise and metallic.

140.

One girl has a circle cut into her belly, another tried to cut her breasts off because she was just fucking tired, another pretends to say "yes" when she knows she doesn't have a choice.

141.

I open my legs and a hard-boiled egg falls out of my cunt. I pretend it is a child.

142.

When she dies we cut up bits of her and use them like flesh soap, red streaks of her kidneys coat our bodies and leave our skin a weird fuchsia.

143.

She pulls a kitchen knife out of the back pocket of her denim jumpsuit and when she bends me over at first I think that she's going to cut my dick off but then she rams it into me and says "What happens in Vegas stays in Vegas" as I writhe like a headless snake under her.

144.

Mike says that "Lesbian" is for ladies with nothing better to do and that a good fuck sets it all righty.

145.

My lips are small animals as she pours her homemade vodka down my throat and then gets out the pliers.

146.

It came bursting out of her in twos, a baby with three heads, four legs and a tail.

147.

The virginity I sort of have weighs against my twenty-nine-year-old thighs. I've tried bars, construction sites, funeral homes, clubs, restaurants, small businesses, hookah bars, no takers, single mingle, prostitutes, candy, escorts, speed dating for your inner bisexual, craigslist, real estate agencies, gyms, carwashes, sex shops. I've tried bondage, nipple piercings, bodycon dresses, platforms, makeup artists, two thousand dollar hair salons. I've taped printouts of bad porn on my clothing. I got a tattoo that says "fuck me." I've tried two hundred shades of red on my lips.

148.

I lick my elbow when I'm unhappy.

149.

I can still feel his body wrapped around my arms every morning.
I wonder what his ashes taste like: the strawberries when we kissed?
His cheap cologne? The ten years of beer every afternoon until
he passed out/blacked out/unknown? I dabble my thumb in his
urn: blackberry pie.

150.

The trackmarks down my thighs remind him of hot corpses.

151.

I don't date girls who talk to Elmo.

152.

He only calls me bro when he's stoned and eating the frozen brownies in my freezer. "Satiated, bro," he says, picking lint out of my dreadlocks. "Bro, that's whacked," I say, eating frozen peas out of the Buddha hand on my wall.

153.

Fucker John and Cookie Monster Rob and I are in the car when I take a safety pin to my ear cartilage.

154.

I was an oracle in the brothel every night.

155.

When the blood first comes I don't cry, or feel like a woman or
girl or in-between person with a vagina, I call 911 and ask for an
ambulance right fucking now please.

156.

I rub her belly, all hard and full and babied up.

157.

When I run out of coke I do heroin. When the heroin is gone I drink nail polish remover. I think of the lacquer of my intestines floating off and running red through me.

158.

His knee socks make me uncomfortable.

159.

They give me the coat of shame for having tits.

160.

The abortionist plays violin and has three cats. Her eyes are the color of the condom wrapper we forgot: dark blue and transparent.

161.

I take photos of the places that I want to change: the crook of an elbow bent too far, the lobe of my ear in the part where the flesh hangs too round, the spaces indented by girth and bone and rippled water skin.

162.

I tried to remove my freckles with milk and bleach.

163.

I wear dildo necklaces. I also wear poodle skirts and draw puppies on my lips.

164.

He named the mole on his breast Claudia.

165.

He moves his hand downwards, his eyelashes and lips prevail against the seal like resistance of skin.

166.

My skin is a galaxy of pus-studded stars.

167.

He thinks her pussy is too loose and suggests dumbbells.

168.

After the needle pushed in too far for two days and counting, my wrists feel like chicken and I cry chemical salt.

169.

Clowns remind her of Him. She writes His name with her nail on her thigh.

170.

Instead of going to homecoming, we go to a bar with Billy-Bob Jones. Ann's pseudocorsage leaves a rash. After Jello shots we go to his trailer and he shows us his *Playboy* collection, and we think about, and then do, take our clothes off.

171.

I cut a thin trail of wrist with her pocketknife.

172.

She swallowed three bullets, an apple, and a pearl earring.

173.

His nose is like a pyramid: dependable, but complex in its architecture.

174.

Her five-year-old tears taste like onions: an old woman beneath the gold of her freckles.

175.

I swallow his citrine stud earring, follow it with a lemon, salt, and a screw from his kitchen floor.

176.

I add a collarbone, iron from the saw, the flesh of his shoulders sliding down my throat, cheap wine. I cut the tip off of my elbow, marinate it in brown sugar and plums.

177.

The kiss tasted like iron and Adderall.

178.

His hands are a soliloquy for limbs themselves.

179.

After the transition, after the Ace bandages, the compression cups, the stitches. Once the strap-on is thrown away he drinks cider in his kitchen, his thumb slips whenever he cuts peppers: a nick to be remembered.

180.

I want to slide a kitchen knife into his barely formed ribs, to slice his singing Broadway mouth open with a letter opener, his small limbs that dangle from trees too dumb to know to break and send his body airborne.

181.

Before she put her head in the oven she sang Thomas the Tank
Engine to her reflection.

182.

He smears red lipstick on his nipples.

183.

The Fire Eater's hands a scalded cobalt, flakes of skin fall from his
violet mouth. It can't go above three hundred degrees, he says, but
once is all it takes and then, when his throat is a scorched oyster
of orange, he will take the telephone and swallow it, cord and plug
and all, and writhe in his own connectedness.

184.

Her Siamese twin is a shadow, a lump protruding from her ribcage that she equates (to her lovers) as a bone break gone awry.

185.

She asked me to choke her, to make the orgasm better, twenty-five and her eyeballs tripping out of their mascara sockets. My hands a question and then a vise. Before her neck turned blue and snapped in my hands, a bird appeared on her chest.

186.

Death-head, he drinks Grey Goose and calls himself Russian. Coils of skin settle on the back of his neck.

187.

Before the baby comes he wants to try anal and go sky diving.
I want to drink the paint in the nursery, to lick it off my teeth and
watch the color drain onto my chest, and lower.

188.

We get wasted for the first time, panting, our heads thrown back,
the tendons of our necks choking with cheap wine and bile.

189.

His eyes are like roadkill, I want to fry and lick the slime off
of them.

190.

My thumbs splay crooked, the places where I was cut stitched crooked down.

191.

She steals cucumbers and root vegetables from the kitchens, says she fucks trees.

192.

Don't date no fuckin' fairies, he tells me, his eyebrows furrow from too many beers, from not enough oxygen, from a truck-driving tobacco-chewing childhood.

193.

The afterbirth is more of a baby than the thing on my floor.

194.

I wrap his hair around my dildo, a sick kind of magic, angry love.

195.

"I put his head in the oven to see what bodies taste like," I tell them in their black suits, with their flashing lights.

196.

I prepare rutabagas, nuts and wine. Add some amphetamines to his glass.

197.

He dropped the ring on a gravestone and didn't pick it up, but I'll marry him anyway, he of the endless khakis.

198.

Do your girlfriends always burn your houses down?

199.

But suddenly a bird appears, a tattoo angry from the needles, and ten different shades of ink spread down her thigh.

200.

She snorted the last of my coke then sang "The Star Spangled Banner."

201.

The horse trampled her and the sweet lemonade in her hands. We all pretended to be surprised.

202.

After the dead baby, I make a hole in the yard for the squirrels to bleed in.

203.

But what they don't know about is the whiskey in my coffee.

204.

He's into silicone breasts and shredded tires.

205.

My mouth is a snail.

206.

He looks downward, at his penis, and pulls on his hoodie and street shoes. This license plate will make them call him the sex machine, he thinks. Grape juice box dangling from his mouth, he steps back and surveys: DICKLRD.

207.

"I don't kiss boys who wear eyeliner," Meagan says, her hair feathered beyond comprehension.

208.

They try to conceal their hard-ons behind lukewarm cups of Fanta.

209.

His wrists are graphs of different metals.

210.

I cry for the way her hands held mugs, and then for the way they touched my face.

211.

His heart is a pulp of gray matter in my latex-covered hands, the places where his breath once was ache purple in the fluorescent light.

212.

His drinking is becoming more fish and less grizzly bear. His mauled red organs. His shallow water breaths.

213.

The junkyard is a sleet of rusted metal, he tears his knee on the fence and asks for warm milk. I wrap the remnants of a couch around his mouth so he can't speak.

214.

My fingers button against his neck, the tendon and vein pulsed into galaxies before a star explodes.

215.

Her mouth a cotton-tailed swamp against my sternum, the hollow of it damp and sad.

216.

The fish of Jesus taste like semen and mud.

217.

I cut my nails with pliers and tear the top of a finger clean off.
I drink a bottle and wear my wife's old shoes, the satin worn thin
and tinted like dishwater.

218.

I find a magazine called *Naughty Boy Boner* in the cabinet where he
keeps his Dover rose china. I put my wedding band in between the
faces of a man in a Santa hat mid-thrust and a man with hair so
long and thick he must be Farrah Fawcett's baby.

219.

I shoot up in my bridal bathrobe, the sequined tie glinting against my arms. I want a stained window lens for when I put on the dress with the sleeves designed to conceal and not embellish, for when I walk down the aisle with my fish-face covered in a lace doily.

220.

I dye my hair the color of the blood on my thighs the first time it arrived.

221.

Her mouth is a slot for me to push stones in. I slip in three.

222.

Mother is a face full of wasp stings from when she batted the nest in her beer can curlers, her eyes covered in last night's liner and Ponds cream, her spray tan a splotched sick animal suffocating her skin.

223.

I fell off the pole before the baby came out, my platforms falling like angry hail, my lipstick a streak on the ground that he can't wash off.

224.

"Suicide is a big fucking decision," he says, stubbing his j-bird out on my flannel shirt.

225.

She's singing "I Kissed a Girl" on my couch now. Her baby's first word was "motherfucker."

226.

He likes boys with dark eyes and scars that don't add up, he calls it flesh algebra.

227.

She put her hand on the space above where I swallow.

228.

He likes toddlers and the shapes their small wormy bodies make. He's the pediatrician in the woods behind your house, the cashier with the cigarette burns, the teacher who looks in one place too long, who hugs too much.

229.

My mouth is a hovercraft.

230.

I want to consume the way the boys shake their hair, their glasses, their pissed off sweaters. The way they can't drive stick, crashing into dumpsters, their unyielding moustache embryo.

231.

Her shoulder is a river for my salty face.

232.

My breasts aren't the same size, first I go for the socks, the tissues, the ball-shaped objects that are stuffable, then I go for the silicone, the surgeon's table, the constant shifting of bra sizes.

233.

He asks if I want to drink his piss.

234.

I take a knife to the insides of my thighs, try to assemble some kind of gap, a space where the skin doesn't meet.

235.

I lick the spaces of her that don't connect.

236.

We watch TV on his mother's couch with the needle-pointed penis cushions. She offers us fruit cake slices. Bits of fur protrude from the edges.

237.

Freak of nature: my eyes change colors when I cry or do speed.

238.

Repetition, I could burn down her apartment, get a bikini wax, join a band where everyone is really good at saying "fuck," or I could cut my hair, change my will, read Proust and drink bad tequila.

239.

He said she was too beautiful to die.

240.

When we get stoned I think that I am a dolphin with pearls for incisors.

241.

I drink milk and vinegar, add a dead moth and grass from his lawn.

242.

Mary says her belly feels weird and we both say "what?" and she says she feels teeth inside of it, then asks if we have E. Her face is shaped like angry moons and the place where a diamond once was in her nose is bleeding and we see white specks of pus or something like it.

243.

I type my name without capitals: a failured existence.

244.

He wants to be spanked before he eats his dinner.

245.

My teeth are rotten from spiked punch, I leave them scattered like fallen planets on the yard of his dilapidated house.

246.

I eat her chickens, butter-drenched, leave their remains on her kitschy gingham table, my stomach pregnant with spray-on oil.

247.

She pierced my ears with a fork.

248.

I got so high I realized that nothing is real except for Jesus's abs and pink glitter glue.

249.

I eat confetti, my mouth a pulpy green mass.

250.

Betty calls me a pyro, my steaming eyes and fishing trips where I come back smelling like driftwood fires. I put Elmers glue in her ears.

251.

I want to swallow his acne, to consume him like a small animal would eat insects.

252.

She needs help buttoning her jeans, my hands squeaking against the rubber of her, the shudder smell that follows her home from the classrooms where she adopts small children who can't speak.

253.

She swallows the turpentine first, then closes the space of my hands in paper cutters, her butter chin quivering with an emotion I don't yet know.

254.

His thumb turns green first, then his forearms and neck, his lips a gray smog. "This is how it ends," he says, fingers hooked in a bed frame from the 1950s.

255.

She wants to be a rainbow sparkle unicorn, sprinkles and nothing else, perpetual lipstick, small-armed kind of girl, but her face is a broken oval.

256.

I haven't eaten for a week and my flesh is beginning to hang off the wire of my joints.

257.

He calls it the witching hour, the time when mirrors turn red and his skin a prick of cold against the down of his bed. He sees swans in her sleeping eyes.

258.

Rum is my mouthwash, she says, leatherneck protruding from the dentist's chair, her canines stabbing out of her gums.

259.

His sparrow neck broke when the ladder was tied wrong, his body a sea of bruises, now he eats only tapioca and Fox News, his chin indignant at the homosexuals and the shapes their mouths are taking. He can't move his arms but keeps a shotgun under his rocker in case of an incident.

260.

Karrie and I stole holy wine and soaked our tampons in it and then got bladder infections. Which, Karrie said, hurt so bad it was worse than giving birth. She would know, because she is the new Virgin Mary. She left to give birth a second time to an invisible man's child and came back to school but not really: hollowed out eyes, stretch marks she won't let us rub cocoa butter on.

261.

Lacy doesn't wear sweaters because she's cold.

262.

She broke me open. Red in my mouth. Sore thighs. I didn't say anything, just drank a glass of lukewarm milk, pulled my underwear back on. The nape of her neck, bloody strands.

263.

After the bird-boned baby, I tied myself to a train track hoping for disaster, the blow of a body and the stains it makes on iron.

264.

His father owned a fish farm and before we fucked but after we
kissed he propped a shotgun between us, said he had a girlfriend,
didn't go for boys. I unbuttoned my shirt. He prayed later.

265.

The spaces we have broken: an arm, eight fingers, three tongues,
one rib cage, the fresh absence of a tramp stamp, the bone before
the wrist, a nose, five shoulders and a silver wrench.

266.

The thing is we are probably angels.

ACKNOWLEDGEMENTS

Excerpts from *Fleshgraphs* have appeared in *The Ink & Code, The Offending Adam, Pine Hills Review, Revolver,* and *Souvenir*. I'd like to thank Keegan Lester, Peter LaBerge, Kazim Ali, Lindsey Boldt, Stephen Motika, everyone at Nightboat Books, my family, Aidan Forster, Blythe King, Isabella Nilsson, and everyone who read the first cut of the manuscript.

ABOUT THE AUTHOR

BRYNNE REBELE-HENRY was born in 1999. Her poetry, fiction, and nonfiction have appeared in *Prairie Schooner, Denver Quarterly, Fiction International, The Volta, So to Speak, Verse,* and *Adroit,* among other publications. She has received numerous honors for her work, including the Louise Louis/Emily F. Bourne Award from the Poetry Society of America and the *Adroit* Prize for Fiction.

NIGHTBOAT BOOKS

Nightboat Books, a nonprofit organization, seeks to develop audiences for writers whose work resists convention and transcends boundaries. We publish books rich with poignancy, intelligence, and risk. Please visit our website, www.nightboat.org, to learn about our titles and how you can support our future publications.

The following individuals have supported the publication of this book. We thank them for their generosity and commitment to the mission of Nightboat Books:

Elizabeth Motika
Benjamin Taylor

In addition, this book has been made possible, in part, by grants from the National Endowment for the Arts and the New York State Council on the Arts Literature Program.

© 2016 by Brynne Rebele-Henry
All rights reserved
Printed in the United States

ISBN 978-1-937658-54-0
Design and typesetting by HR Hegnauer
Text set in Mrs Eaves

Cataloging-in-publication data is available
from the Library of Congress

Distributed by University Press of New England
One Court Street
Lebanon, NH 03766
www.upne.com

Nightboat Books
New York
www.nightboat.org